GEO

J

TOP 10 AFRICAN-AMERICAN MEN'S ATHLETES

Jeff Savage

SPORTS TOP 10

Enslow Publishers, Inc.

40 Industrial Road   PO Box 38
Box 398   Aldershot
Berkeley Heights, NJ 07922   Hants GU12 6BP
USA   UK

http://www.enslow.com

Library of Congress Cataloging-in-Publication Data

Savage, Jeff, 1961–
    Top 10 African-American men's athletes / Jeff Savage.
       p. cm. — (Sports top 10)
    Includes bibliographical references and index.
    ISBN 0-7660-1494-0
    1. Athletes—United States—Biography—Juvenile literature.
2. Afro-American athletes—Biography—Juvenile literature.
3. Afro-American athletes—Rating of—Juvenile literature. [1. Athletes.
2. Afro-Americans—Biography.] I. Title: Top ten African-American
men's athletes. II. Title. III. Sports top 10.
GV697.A1 S328 2001
796'.092'396073—dc21

                               00-012335

Printed in the United States of America

10 9 8 7 6 5 4 3 2 1

To Our Readers: We have done our best to make sure all Internet addresses in this
book were active and appropriate when we went to press. However, the author and
the publisher have no control over and assume no liability for the material available
on those Internet sites or on other Web sites they may link to. Any comments or
suggestions can be sent by e-mail to comments@enslow.com or to the address on
the back cover.

Illustration Credits: Andrew D. Bernstein/NBA Photos, pp. 7, 9; Andy Hayt/NBA
Photos, p. 22; AP\Wide World Photos, pp. 31, 33; International Tennis Hall of Fame
and Museum, pp. 14, 17; Lou Capozzola, NBA Photos, p. 25; National Baseball Hall
of Fame Library Cooperstown, N.Y., pp. 35, 37; National Football League Properties,
Inc., pp. 18, 21; Rich Pecjak, pp. 38, 41; The *Ring*, pp. 11, 13, 27, 29; United States Golf
Association/J. D. Cuban, p. 45; United States Golf Association/John Mummert, p. 42.

Cover Illustration: Nathaniel S. Butler/NBA Photos.

Cover Description: Michael Jordan.

CONTENTS

INTRODUCTION

AFRICAN-AMERICAN ATHLETES have flourished in sports for many years. There was a time not long ago in America, however, when African Americans were ignored or even prohibited from competing simply because of the color of their skin. Overcoming an opponent on the field of play is one thing; overcoming racism is quite another.

The ten African-American men chosen for this book may not necessarily be the ten greatest athletes to have ever lived in the United States. Other factors raised their stature in our eyes, such as their off-the-field impact on the sports world or their contribution to the sport in which they played.

For instance, there are many great African-American baseball players, such as Barry Bonds and Ken Griffey, Jr. today, and Willie Mays and Hank Aaron from a generation before. But Jackie Robinson has been selected as the representative for baseball. We have chosen Robinson not just because of his greatness in the field, particularly on the base paths, but because in 1947 he broke the game's color barrier by becoming the first African American to play major-league baseball in the twentieth century.

In Olympic track, several African-American sprinters and jumpers have captured the spotlight. Certainly, Carl Lewis cannot be ignored for his record nine gold medals, as well as Michael Johnson's performance at the 1996 Olympics. Jesse Owens was chosen, though, because of the social impact his four-gold-medal performance at the 1936 Berlin Olympics had on Adolf Hitler's racist movement in Germany.

Muhammad Ali was the first person to be heavyweight champion three times, and his social impact on sports during the Civil Rights era of the 1960s is unmatched.

In the last half century, basketball has been dominated by three centers: Wilt Chamberlain, Bill Russell, and

Kareem Abdul-Jabbar. We have selected Abdul-Jabbar for his collegiate dominance, his longevity, and his contributions to the game, such as the revolutionary sky hook.

In football, such African-American running backs as Walter Payton, Barry Sanders, and Emmitt Smith have gained more yardage than Jim Brown. We have chosen Brown over the others because of his dominance before retiring at the age of thirty. Likewise, our other football choice, Deion Sanders, may not be the second-best African-American pro football player ever, but he is the only person with both an interception and a pass reception in a Super Bowl and he is the only person to have played in both a Super Bowl and a World Series.

With so many great African-American athletes, it is nearly impossible to pick ten men. There are many others who are deserving to be listed among the best. The ten we have selected certainly stand out, but perhaps you can think of others. Here is *our* top ten list.

CAREER STATISTICS

ATHLETE	SPORT	GREATEST ACHIEVEMENT
KAREEM ABDUL-JABBAR	BASKETBALL	NBA ALL-STAR 19 TIMES
MUHAMMAD ALI	BOXING	THREE-TIME HEAVYWEIGHT CHAMPION
ARTHUR ASHE	TENNIS	WIMBLEDON AND U.S. OPEN CHAMPION
JIM BROWN	FOOTBALL	LED NFL IN RUSHING EIGHT TIMES
MICHAEL JORDAN	BASKETBALL	BEST PER-GAME SCORING AVERAGE EVER
JOE LOUIS	BOXING	HELD HEAVYWEIGHT TITLE LONGER THAN ANYONE
JESSE OWENS	TRACK & FIELD	WON FOUR GOLD MEDALS AT OLYMPICS
JACKIE ROBINSON	BASEBALL	BROKE BASEBALL'S COLOR BARRIER
DEION SANDERS	BASEBALL/FOOTBALL	PLAYED IN SUPER BOWL AND WORLD SERIES
TIGER WOODS	GOLF	RECORDS IN ALL FOUR GRAND SLAM EVENTS

Kareem Abdul-Jabbar

KAREEM ABDUL-JABBAR HAD THE BALL DOWN LOW. Boston Celtics center Robert Parish pushed into him from behind. Larry Bird and Kevin McHale pawed at the ball in front. Abdul-Jabbar turned in one sweeping motion and lifted the ball in his right hand more than ten feet in the air and released it off his fingertips so that it traveled sloping down to the basket. The Celtics were not allowed to touch it; doing so would be a goaltending violation. They could only hope that it did not go through the hoop, but it did. The Los Angeles Lakers were now on their way to winning the 1985 NBA Championship.

Kareem Abdul-Jabbar was born in New York City as Ferdinand Lewis Alcindor, Jr. He went by the name Lew, and did not change his name until age twenty-four. He was the only child of Al and Cora Alcindor, a transit policeman and a homemaker. The Alcindors lived in a housing project in Harlem where Lew spent most hours indoors doing his homework and listening to his father's jazz music.

Lew Alcindor's favorite sport growing up was baseball, and by fifth grade he was a power pitcher whose occasional wildness scared his Little League opponents and their parents. "I can remember seeing some parents cringing," he said, "as their sons in the batter's box ducked and leaped away from some of the heat I was throwing."[1] By seventh grade Alcindor had grown tall enough to touch a basketball rim, and his fingers were long enough to palm a basketball, and so he changed sports. By the end of his eighth-grade year he was one inch short of seven feet.

Alcindor was the starting center all four years at Power

KAREEM ABDUL-JABBAR

Kareem Abdul-Jabbar created his signature move, "the sky hook", while playing college basketball at UCLA.

Memorial High School in downtown Manhattan. He wept openly in the locker room after he lost his first high school game, but there were few occasions to cry after that. Power Memorial went undefeated his sophomore and junior seasons and lost just once his final year there. Alcindor was a three-time high school All-America selection and the most heavily recruited player in the country.

Alcindor chose UCLA, which had just emerged as a basketball power under coach John Wooden. At that time, freshmen were not allowed to play varsity college basketball, but in the next three seasons Alcindor led the Bruins to records of 30–0, 29–1, and 29–1, and three straight NCAA championships. He brought the slam dunk to the forefront of modern basketball. Then, when the NCAA banned the dunk in 1967, his junior year, he responded by creating the unstoppable sky hook.

Alcindor was the first player chosen in the 1969 NBA draft (by the Milwaukee Bucks, an expansion team that had lost fifty-five games the year before). Alcindor immediately changed the fortunes of the Bucks by scoring 29 points in his first pro game, eventually averaging 28.8 for the year. Milwaukee finished the season, 56–26. Alcindor also changed his name to Kareem Abdul-Jabbar, which is Islamic for "generous and powerful servant of Allah."

After leading the Bucks to the 1971 NBA title, Abdul-Jabbar toiled in Milwaukee for four more seasons before being traded to the Los Angeles Lakers. At seven feet, two inches, and wearing goggles, Abdul-Jabbar stood out on the court and became a fan favorite. Teaming with Magic Johnson to form a run-and-gun offense called "Showtime," Abdul-Jabbar and the Lakers won five NBA titles in the 1980s. "He always looked like he was playing to music," said Johnson. "The things he did were unheard of for centers. He won and he did it with style."[2]

KAREEM ABDUL-JABBAR

BORN: April 16, 1947, New York, New York.

HIGH SCHOOL: Power Memorial High School, Manhattan, New York.

COLLEGE: UCLA.

PRO: Milwaukee Bucks, 1969–1975; Los Angeles Lakers, 1975–1989.

RECORDS: Holds NBA career records for most points scored (38,387), field goals made (15,837) and attempted (28,307); second all time in games played (1,560); third all-time in rebounds (17,440).

HONORS: Only college player to win three Final Four Most Outstanding Player awards while winning three national titles, 1967–1969; NBA Rookie of the Year, 1970; six-time NBA Most Valuable Player, 1971–1972, 1974, 1976–1977, 1980; six-time member of NBA championship team, 1971, 1980, 1982, 1985, 1987–1988; named to NBA All-Star team 19 times; elected to Naismith Memorial Basketball Hall of Fame, 1995.

Abdul-Jabbar was the first player chosen in the 1969 NBA draft. He played with the Milwaukee Bucks before being traded to the Los Angeles Lakers prior to the 1975–1976 season.

Internet Address

http://www.hoophall.com/halloffamers/Abdul-Jabbar.htm

SONNY LISTON WAS THE HEAVYWEIGHT CHAMPION of the world. He had polished boxing skills and a powerful wallop. Experts called him "a virtually indestructible and demonstrably deadly fighting machine."[1] So when a brash-talking youngster named Cassius Clay entered the ring on February 25, 1964, in Miami, Florida, most people predicted a quick knockout.

Instead, Clay danced and glided around Liston to avoid the champion's punches. He poked jabs at the champ. Liston could not keep up. By the third round, everyone could see that the champ was in trouble. Clay had described his boxing style with poetic lines such as, "float like a butterfly, sting like a bee . . ."[2] and he was showing the world that it was so. Finally, Liston took a seat in his corner after the sixth round and did not stand back up.

Muhammad Ali was born in Louisville, Kentucky, as Cassius Clay, Jr., the older of two sons of Cassius and Odessa Clay. One day when Cassius Clay was twelve years old, his bicycle was stolen outside an auditorium. He was told to go to the basement and report it to a policeman who was giving boxing lessons. Clay began attending the lessons regularly.

Over Clay's amateur career he won 100 of 105 bouts, and at the 1960 Olympics in Rome, Italy, he won the gold medal in the light heavyweight division. Expecting to return home to Kentucky to a hero's welcome, he instead was challenged to fights by ignorant bigots. After an incident with a motorcycle gang leader, he threw his Olympic gold medal into the Ohio River.

MUHAMMAD ALI

Today Muhammad Ali suffers from Parkinson's disease. Although he retired from boxing in 1980, he still has one of the most recognizable faces in the world.

Later that year, Clay turned pro. In 1964, he stunned the world with his victory over Liston. Shortly afterward, Clay professed his faith to Islam and changed his name to Muhammad Ali. In his rematch with Liston the following year, Ali retained his title with a first-round knockout. He successfully defended his title several times over the next two years. Then, in 1967, he refused, on religious grounds, to be inducted into the U.S. Army and join the war in Vietnam. He was stripped of his heavyweight title and barred from boxing.

Finally, forty-three months after he was barred, Ali sued in court and won the right to box again. He fought Jerry Quarry and won. He struggled against Oscar Bonavena but won again. Then, in perhaps the most celebrated match of all time, he met Joe Frazier at Madison Square Garden in New York in 1971. Frazier was heavyweight champion and beat Ali, by decision, in 15 rounds.

Ali won a series of bouts after that, and then in 1974 avenged his loss to Frazier (who had since lost the title belt to George Foreman). This gave Ali a shot at the champion Foreman. In a match in Zaire, Africa, billed as the "Rumble in the Jungle," Ali used a tactic he created called the rope-a-dope. He leaned against the ropes and covered his face and allowed Foreman to punch repeatedly. By the eighth round, Foreman was exhausted from throwing so many punches. Ali's energy level was still high, and he scored a knockout and reclaimed the heavyweight title. He beat Frazier again in the "Thrilla in Manila" and won many more bouts before losing in 1978 to Leon Spinks. He reclaimed the title from Spinks later that year.

Today Ali suffers from Parkinson's disease, and his speech and movement are quite slow. Yet many people still say he has the most recognizable face in the world.

BORN: January 18, 1942, Louisville, Kentucky.

HIGH SCHOOL: Central High School, Louisville, Kentucky.

TURNED PRO: 1960.

RECORDS: Amateur record of 100–5; pro record of 56–5 with 37 knockouts; first boxer ever to win the world heavyweight championship three times, 1964, 1974, 1978.

HONORS: Six-time Kentucky amateur Golden Gloves champion; Olympic gold medalist, 1960; three-time world champion lasting nine years, 1964–1967, 1974–1978; inducted into International Boxing Hall of Fame, 1990.

In 1964 Cassius Clay, otherwise known as Muhammad Ali, exploded into the world of professional boxing when he beat heavyweight champion Sonny Liston.

Internet Address

http://www.ibhof.com/ali.htm

ARTHUR ASHE

When Arthur Ashe beat Jimmy Connors in the 1975 Wimbledon championship, he proved that he was not only a spokesperson for social causes, but also a great tennis player.

ARTHUR ASHE HAD TO FIND A WAY to defeat Jimmy
Connors. Few in the Wimbledon crowd at the All-England
Club gave him a chance. Connors was the top-ranked player
in the world and the defending Wimbledon champion.
Ashe was an accomplished player as well, but he was better
known as a dignified spokesperson for social causes. Did he
have the courage and will to win the 1975 Wimbledon title?

Ashe proved his tennis greatness. With a hard serve and
attacking style, he stunned Connors by sweeping the first
two sets by identical 6–1 scores. Connors rallied to win the
third set, and now the pressure was on. Ashe stood tall and
took the fourth set, 6–4, to win the title. Ashe made a con-
scious effort never to show emotion on the court, but upon
capturing match point against Connors, he turned to the
players' box where his friends were seated and pumped his
fist in victory. Then he reached across the net to shake his
opponent's hand.

Arthur Ashe grew up in Richmond, Virginia, the first of
two children of Arthur, Sr., and Mattie Ashe. One Sunday
morning just before Arthur turned seven, his father sat
down on the bottom bunk bed between Arthur and his
brother, Johnnie, and told them that their mother had died
during the night. "My father was a strong, dutiful, provid-
ing man," said Ashe. "From that time on he was father and
mother to us."[1]

One day when he was seven, Arthur had been standing
behind the fence next door at the Brook Field Playground
for an hour. He was watching Ron Charity, the best

African-American tennis player in Richmond, practice his serve alone on one of the courts. Charity calmly approached Arthur and said, "Would you like to learn to play?" Arthur smiled and said, "Yes, I would."[2] Over the next two years, Charity taught Arthur the basics of the game.

As a teenager, Arthur won a string of junior tournaments and gained a scholarship to UCLA. He won the NCAA singles and doubles championships in 1965 before graduating a year later with a degree in business administration.

In 1963, Ashe became the first African American to play for the U.S. Davis Cup team, in which different countries compete in singles and doubles matches to win a prized trophy. Ashe led the United States to the Cup title and played on the team for the next ten years. The 1968 U.S. Open at Forest Hills marked Ashe's breakthrough when he became the first African-American male to win a Grand Slam tournament. Two years later he won another of the four Grand Slam events, the Australian Open, with a straight sets victory in the final.

Ashe was far more than a tennis player. His thoughtful manner and sage advice made him a shining beacon to millions. In fact, Ashe had such an impact on America and the world that nearly thirty years after his triumph at the U.S. Open, in 1997, the new home for the tournament in Flushing Meadows was named Arthur Ashe Stadium. However, Ashe was not alive to receive this honor. He had suffered from various illnesses, beginning in 1979 when he had a heart attack. He retired from tennis, yet stayed close to the game by being captain of the U.S. Davis Cup team. In 1992, Ashe announced to the world that he had AIDS. He described how he had contracted HIV from a transfusion of tainted blood several years earlier during a heart bypass operation. He had kept the secret with his family until now. Less than a year later, at the age of forty-nine, Ashe died of pneumonia.

ARTHUR ASHE

BORN: July 10, 1943, Richmond, Virginia.

DIED: February 6, 1993.

HIGH SCHOOL: Walker High School, Richmond, Virginia; Sumner
High School, St. Louis, Missouri (senior year).

COLLEGE: UCLA.

RECORDS: First African-American male to win a Grand Slam tournament (U.S. Open), 1968; first player to win $100,000 in a year,
1970.

HONORS: NCAA singles and doubles champion, 1965; won 33
singles titles, including three Grand Slam tournaments (1968
U.S. Open, 1970 Australian Open, 1975 Wimbledon); inducted
into the International Tennis Hall of Fame, 1985.

Over the course of his tennis career, Ashe won three of the four
grand-slam events.

Internet Address

http://www.tennisfame.com/enshrinees/arthur_ashe.html

JIM BROWN

Jim Brown was always a star. In high school he set records in football, track, lacrosse, baseball, and basketball.

THE BALL WAS AT THE DALLAS COWBOYS 3-yard line. It was fourth down. The score was tied, 3–3, in the second quarter, and the Cleveland Browns decided to go for a touchdown. Everyone at the game in Dallas knew what was coming next. Jim Brown took the handoff and headed left where he was met by three Cowboys. From the 10-yard line, where the Cowboys appeared to have him hemmed in, Brown lowered his head and charged forward. Dave Edwards wrapped both arms around Brown's legs, but the fullback dragged the defender across the 5-yard line. Brown met three more Cowboys in front of the goal line. Together they hit him at once. Brown sent them flying like bowling pins as he lunged into the end zone for the touchdown. It was another amazing run by the man many still consider the best pro running back ever.

Jim Brown was born on St. Simon Island, Georgia, to Swinton and Theresa Brown. His father was a professional boxer who left the family when Jim was a young boy. His mother moved to New York and left Jim in the care of his grandmother and great-grandmother. When Jim was seven he was sent to Long Island to rejoin his mother.

Brown was a star athlete at Manhasset High School where he set school and league records in football, track, lacrosse, baseball, and basketball. A fine student as well, he was offered scholarships by forty-two colleges, and he chose Syracuse University in New York.

In college, Brown starred at track and field and lacrosse, but football was his main sport. He was so dedicated to the game that he passed up a spot on the U.S. Olympic track team, saying, "It wouldn't have been fair. I was in Syracuse on a football scholarship, and the Olympics would have cut into the time I was committed to give to football."[1] Brown was a threat to score anytime, from anywhere on the field. In 1957, he led the Orangemen to the Cotton Bowl where he scored three touchdowns in a 28–27 loss to Texas Christian University. After college, Brown was drafted by the NBA's Syracuse Nationals and the NFL's Cleveland Browns. He chose football.

In a game early in his rookie year, Brown proved worthy of the top pick in the draft, when he rushed for a then-NFL record 237 yards. He finished the season as football's leading rusher, and coaches were already calling him the best running back in the history of the game. Brown's collisions with defenders were legendary. As he approached defenders, he simply lowered his head and crashed into them like a bull. And even though Brown was involved in many violent collisions over nine seasons, he never missed a game. In 1963 he became the highest-paid player in the NFL, earning a yearly salary of $45,000. He also entered the world of movie acting, appearing in such dramas as the Civil War film *Rio Honchos*.

Brown won the rushing title in eight of the nine years he played. In what turned out to be his final season, in 1965, he ran for 1,544 yards, 17 touchdowns, and a per-carry average of 5.4 yards, his best ever. In the summer of 1966, Brown was in London, England, filming the war movie *The Dirty Dozen*. On July 13 he announced that he was retiring from pro football. "I quit with regret but no sorrow," he told a small gathering of reporters. "I've been able to do all the things I wanted to do, and now I want to devote my time to other things."[2] Brown was only thirty years old when he left the game. Had he played several more years, as he was capable of doing, his NFL rushing records would have been as hard to catch as he was.

JIM BROWN

BORN: February 17, 1936, St. Simon Island, Georgia.

HIGH SCHOOL: Manhasset High School, Manhasset, New York.

COLLEGE: Syracuse University.

PRO: Cleveland Browns, 1957–1965.

RECORDS: Set NFL records (since broken) for most yards rushing in a season (1,863), 1963, and a career (12,312); led NFL in rushing eight times.

HONORS: NCAA First-team All-American, 1956; NFL Rookie of the Year, 1957; eight-time All-Pro, 1957–1961, 1963–1965; three-time NFL Most Valuable Player, 1958, 1963, 1965; inducted into College Football Hall of Fame, 1956; enshrined in Pro Football Hall of Fame, 1971.

Sweeping around the end, Jim Brown (32) looks to outrun would-be tacklers.

Internet Address

http://www.profootballhof.com/players/enshrinees/jbrown.cfm

MICHAEL JORDAN

Splitting the defense, Michael Jordan creates room for his shot.

THE CHICAGO BULLS WERE IN TROUBLE. It was Game 6 of the 1998 NBA Finals in Salt Lake City. The Bulls trailed the Utah Jazz by one point, 86–85, with twenty seconds left. Trouble was, the Bulls did not have the ball, the Jazz did. The Bulls were desperate.

Michael Jordan hurried over to Utah's baseline where all-star Karl Malone had the ball. Jordan slapped the ball out of Malone's hands and stole it. Now the Bulls had a chance. The clocked ticked below ten seconds as Jordan held the ball near his free-throw line. He dribbled and juked defender Bryon Russell to create space. Then he elevated from 18 feet away from the basket and released the shot. Good! Jordan's last shot of his amazing pro basketball career had given his team another championship.

Michael Jordan was the fourth of five children born to James and Delores Jordan. He grew up with his family in Wilmington, North Carolina. Michael was not always a great basketball player. In fact, he was cut from the Laney High School varsity team as a sophomore and had to play on the JV team. By his senior year, however, he led Laney to a 19-win season.

Jordan accepted a basketball scholarship to the University of North Carolina at his mother's request. He was a starter as a freshman, and he made an immediate impact for the Tar Heels. He hit the winning shot in the 1982 NCAA Championship Game to defeat Georgetown. He was the College Player of the Year as a sophomore, and then after one more season, announced that he was going pro. He was the third player selected in the 1984 draft, by the floundering Chicago Bulls.

Then the magic began. In a career of memorable moments, Jordan's greatness was unmatched. In a 1986 first-round playoff game against the mighty Boston Celtics and Larry Bird, Jordan scored 63 points to force two over-times at the Boston Garden before the Celtics prevailed, 135–131. "I couldn't believe anybody could do that against the Boston Celtics," said Bird.[1]

Three years later, the Bulls reached the Eastern Conference Finals for the first time. Jordan got them there with "The Shot." It happened in the final game of the first round at Cleveland against the Cavaliers. The Bulls trailed by one point with three seconds left when Jordan told his teammates during a timeout not to worry, that he would hit the winning shot. Sure enough, Jordan hung in midair between two defenders and drained a clutch fifteen-footer. "I just can't believe he made that shot," said Cavaliers center Brad Daugherty. "I don't see how he stayed in the air that long. It's the most outstanding shot I've ever seen."[2]

Jordan shocked the sports world in 1993 when he announced his retirement from basketball to pursue a base-ball career. Jordan joined the Chicago White Sox but did not go beyond the minor-league level.

Jordan ceremoniously rejoined the Bulls late in the 1995 season. In just his fifth game back, he scored a league-high 55 points to lead the Bulls to a 113–111 win over the New York Knicks. Two seasons later, he carried the Bulls to their fifth NBA championship, overcoming the flu in Game 5 of the Finals against the Utah Jazz to score 38 points and nail the winning three-point shot. A year later, in his final pro game, he scored 45 points against the Jazz, stole the ball, and hit the game-winner one last time.

MICHAEL JORDAN

BORN: February 17, 1963, Brooklyn, New York.

HIGH SCHOOL: Laney High School, Wilmington, North Carolina.

COLLEGE: University of North Carolina.

PRO: Chicago Bulls, 1984–1993, 1995–1999.

RECORDS: Career scoring average of 31.5 points per game; led the NBA in scoring ten times; most consecutive games scoring 10 or more points (840).

HONORS: NCAA Player of the Year, 1983; member of six NBA championship teams; five-time NBA Most Valuable Player; six-time NBA Finals Most Valuable Player; named ESPN's Greatest Athlete of the Century, 2000.

At the height of his career, Michael Jordon was one the world's biggest celebrities. He starred in commercials and even a movie.

Internet Address

http://espn.go.com/sportscentury/features/00016048.html

JOE LOUIS

JOE LOUIS, KNOWN TO FANS AS THE BROWN BOMBER, said he entered the boxing ring at Yankee Stadium as excited as "a racehorse in the starting gate."[1] Dozens of reporters sat ringside at their typewriters, and behind them were more than seventy thousand people. Millions more were tuned to radios around the world. It was June 22, 1938. Dictator Adolf Hitler had been proclaiming a "master race" in Germany. Max Schmeling, Louis's opponent, was a German who represented Hitler's claim, even if Schmeling did not believe it himself. What is more, Schmeling had already beaten Louis two years earlier. This bout was a moment of truth for the American public.

At the bell, Louis tore into Schmeling. Just one minute into the fight, Schmeling sagged into the ropes. His trainer threw a white towel into the ring, indicating that Schmeling's camp was quitting the fight. The referee tossed the towel aside because no such rule existed with the New York Boxing Commission. The bout would be over soon enough. Louis continued to pepper Schmeling with a barrage of punches, repeatedly knocking the German to the canvas. Finally, Schmeling could not get back up, and he was counted out. The fight lasted only two minutes and four seconds. There was dancing in America's streets, and Louis was a hero.

Joe Louis Barrow was the seventh of eight children born to Munn and Lillie Barrow. The family lived in a two-room house on the red clay hills of eastern Alabama. Together they tilled the soil, grew the cotton, picked it, packed it up, and sold it. By the time Joe Louis was twelve, his mother

JOE LOUIS

In 1938 Joe Louis became a national hero when he defeated the German boxer, Max Schmeling. By knocking out Schmeling, Louis championed for African-Americans, as well as all of America.

had divorced, remarried, and moved the family north to Detroit, Michigan. Louis was overwhelmed by city life. He was seventeen when he was introduced to boxing by a friend at Brewster's East Side Gymnasium. Louis began training every day. Soon after, in late 1932, he lost his first amateur fight in two rounds. Then he started winning.

Louis turned pro in 1934 and set off on an incredible prize-fighting journey. In June 1936, he lost at Yankee Stadium when Schmeling knocked him out in the twelfth round. Now Louis was more determined than ever. A year later, in June 1937, he beat James Braddock with an eighth-round knockout to win the heavyweight title. Afterward came a run of twenty-five title defenses over a twelve-year stretch—the longest reign of a heavyweight champion in history. Through it all, Louis's kindness outside the ring endeared him to Americans of all races, who faithfully listened to radio broadcasts of all his fights.

On January 10, 1942, Louis enlisted in the Army. His show of support stirred the nation. As one biographer wrote: "To a country deeply divided along racial lines, yet desperately wanting to believe it was united against a common foe, Louis [became] a symbol of national unity."[2] For the next four years, Louis traveled around the country visiting Army bases and inspiring troops.

Louis was discharged from the Army in October 1945, at which time he resumed defense of his heavyweight title. After recording two knockouts at Yankee Stadium in the summer and fall of 1946, he won a split decision over Jersey Joe Walcott. Fans clamored for a rematch, and Louis and Walcott obliged by meeting at Yankee Stadium in June 1948. This time there was no doubt as Louis knocked out Walcott in the eleventh round. The Brown Bomber retired from boxing, then returned to the ring briefly before retiring for good in 1951.

Joe Louis

Born: May 13, 1914, Lafayette, Alabama.

Died: April 12, 1981.

High School: Bronson Trade School, Detroit, Michigan.

Turned Pro: 1934.

Records: Pro record of 71–3 with 54 KOs; Defended his heavyweight title twenty-five times; held heavyweight title for eleven years and eight months—longest consecutive reign in history.

Honors: Inducted into International Boxing Hall of Fame, 1990.

Louis and Arturo Godoy square off in this 1940 bout. From 1937 to 1942, Louis defended his title twenty five times, the longest reign of any heavyweight champion in history.

Internet Address

http://espn.go.com/sportscentury/features/00016109.html

JESSE OWENS

JESSE OWENS PACED NERVOUSLY ON THE TRACK. Owens had just fouled on his second of three qualifying attempts at the long jump. It was the 1936 Olympic Games in Berlin, Germany, where dictator Adolf Hitler was proclaiming a "master race" for his countrymen. To Hitler's way of thinking, Owens represented an "inferior" race. Owens knew what his performance at these Games meant to the world.

German long jumper Luz Long approached Owens and said, "What has taken your goat?"[1] Owens smiled at the German's awkward use of the English language, but he knew what Long meant. Many Germans did not agree with Hitler's bigotry, and Long was among them. He suggested that Owens place a white towel a few inches behind the foul board to mark a new take-off spot. It worked. Owens qualified and then beat Long in the final for the gold medal. Long hugged Owens as 110,000 German fans chanted "Jazze Owenz! JAZZE OWENZ!"[2] At the spectacle, Hitler left his box and fled the stadium. Owens went on to claim a record four gold medals at the Games, exploding Hitler's myth of supremacy in the process.

James Cleveland Owens was the last of nine children born to Henry and Emma Owens in a small, poor town in northern Alabama. As a child, "J. C.," as he was known, worked in the cotton fields and never noticed the poverty around him. When his elementary school teacher asked his name on his first day of school, he answered "J. C.," in his southern accent. The teacher heard it as "Jesse," and asked. him if this was correct. "J. C., ma'am," he said. "Jesse?" she

JESSE OWENS

By winning four gold medals at the 1936 Olympics in Berlin, Germany, Jesse Owens proved to Hitler and the world that there was no such thing as an inferior race.

asked. "Yes, ma'am," he said. And his name became Jesse Owens.[3]

Fairview Junior High School track and field coach Charles Riley took a profound interest in Owens. He often came to school with breakfast for Jesse, and sometimes took him home for lunch or dinner. Jesse called Riley "Pop," and described him as "a rare man, as much a father to me as Henry Owens was."[4]

When Jesse soared 6 feet in the high jump and nearly 23 feet in the long jump to break the American record for junior high schools, he and his coach sensed greatness. Jesse enrolled at East Technical High School, and Riley stayed with him, refining his running and jumping skills. At the 1933 National Interscholastic Championships track and field meet, Jesse won the 100-yard dash in 9.4 seconds. He also won the 200-yard dash in 20.7 seconds, and the long jump at 24 feet, $9\frac{5}{8}$ inches.

Owens chose to enroll at Ohio State University out of loyalty to his home state. It was not easy for Owens to live in Columbus, Ohio, in the 1930s. As an African American, he was not allowed to live in the student dormitory, nor permitted in most restaurants and movie theaters around town.

Under the tutelage of Buckeyes coach Larry Snyder, Owens's college career took off in 1935. At the Big Ten Championship meet in Ann Arbor, Michigan, Owens broke four world records in the span of one hour. He set new marks in the 100-yard and 220-yard dashes, the 220-yard low hurdles, and the long jump.

After his triumphant performance at the Olympic Games, Owens returned to the United States a hero and was given a ticker-tape parade down Broadway in New York City. In 1976, he received the Presidential Medal of Freedom, the highest nonmilitary award that an American citizen can be given.

JESSE OWENS

BORN: September 12, 1913, Oakville, Alabama.

HIGH SCHOOL: East Technical High School, Cleveland, Ohio.

COLLEGE: Ohio State University.

RECORD: Tied world record in the 100-meters (10.3 seconds), and set world records in the 200-meters (20.7 seconds), long jump (26 feet, 5¼ inches), and 4 x 100-meter relay (39.8 seconds) at Olympics, 1936.

HONORS: Four-time Olympic gold-medal winner, 1936; inducted into the National Track & Field Hall of Fame, 1974; inducted into the U.S. Olympic Hall of Fame, 1983.

At the Big Ten Championships in 1935, Owens broke four world records in one hour, stunning the twelve thousand spectators into silence.

Internet Address

http://www.jesseowens.com/

JACKIE ROBINSON

FROM THE END OF THE 1800S until the year 1945, there was one group of players that was not allowed to play major-league baseball, no matter how qualified they were. That group was African Americans. Jackie Robinson changed all that. In 1945 he became the first African American in the twentieth century to be offered a contract by a Major League Baseball team. After a year in the minors, the Brooklyn Dodgers called him up as an infielder in 1947.

Jack Roosevelt Robinson was born in Cairo, Georgia, the youngest child of Jerry and Mallie Robinson. When Jackie was sixteen months old, his mother moved him, his sister, and three brothers to Pasadena, California. Jackie emerged as a star athlete at Muir Tech High where he played shortstop and catcher in baseball, quarterback in football, and guard in basketball. He also competed in the broad jump and pole vault in track and field and even won a prestigious boys' tennis tournament.

Jackie followed in the footsteps of his older brother, Mack, who competed in the 1936 Olympics in Berlin, Germany. The entire Robinson household gathered around a radio to hear the broadcast of the 200-meter race from Europe. The winner was the great Jesse Owens. The silver medal went to Mack Robinson.

Jackie Robinson attended Pasadena Junior College and then UCLA where he was a four-sport athlete. In football he was a quality running back and also led the nation in punt returns. In his first college baseball game he stole five bases, including home. In track he won the NCAA title in

JACKIE ROBINSON

In 1947 Jackie Robinson made history when he became the first African American to play in Major League Baseball.

the broad jump. After college he joined a semi-professional football team before getting drafted into the Army in 1942.

In 1945 Robinson played baseball for the Negro League Kansas City Monarchs and hit .387. Brooklyn Dodgers owner Branch Rickey took notice and signed Robinson to a minor-league contract on October 23, 1945. Robinson was assigned to the minor-league Triple-A Montreal club. After a successful season in Montreal, Robinson signed a major-league contract to play for the Dodgers. That is when the trouble really started.

Opposing managers and players yelled terrible things at Robinson from the dugout. People in the stands hurled objects at him. He was not allowed in certain places such as restaurants and hotels because of the color of his skin. He received death threats in the mail. The pressure on Jackie Robinson was immense, but he never showed his anger.

Major-league baseball players and fans were not the only ones watching Robinson. So were the players in the Negro Leagues, who were eager to show their greatness in the majors. "We were concerned," said star outfielder Monte Irvin of the Newark Eagles. "We read the reports in the paper and heard them on the radio. . . . We were pulling for him. We knew it would open doors for us."[1] Under tremendous pressure, Robinson refused to cave in. "Anybody who says I can't make it," he said, "doesn't know what I've gone through and what I'm prepared to go through to stay up."[2]

Robinson finished the season with a .311 average and 29 steals, more than twice as many as anyone else. He was voted the National League Rookie of the Year. Two years later he was the National League's Most Valuable Player. Robinson stole home twenty times in his career, including once in the 1955 World Series. In 1997, Major League Baseball announced it was retiring Robinson's jersey number forty-two on all teams.

JACKIE ROBINSON

BORN: January 31, 1919, Cairo, Georgia.

DIED: October 24, 1972.

HIGH SCHOOL: John Muir Technical High School, Pasadena, California.

COLLEGE: UCLA.

PRO: Brooklyn Dodgers, 1947–1956.

RECORDS: First African American to play in the major leagues in the twentieth century, 1947.

HONORS: National League Rookie of the Year, 1947; National League Most Valuable Player, 1949; inducted into the National Baseball Hall of Fame, 1962; jersey number forty-two is retired by baseball, 1997.

During his first season in the Brooklyn Dodgers, Robinson was under tremendous pressure to perform. Although the season was rocky at first, Robinson pulled through and was named Rookie of the Year.

Internet Address

http://baseballhalloffame.org/hofers_and_honorees/hofer_bios/rob inson_jackie.htm

DEION SANDERS

At one time or another in high school or college, Deion Sanders starred in baseball, basketball, football, and track and field.

DEION SANDERS STOOD IN THE OUTFIELD in Pittsburgh, Pennsylvania, wearing an Atlanta Braves uniform. He was playing in the 1992 National League Championship Series against the Pittsburgh Pirates. Fifteen hours later he was standing on a football field 1,168 miles away in Miami, Florida, wearing an Atlanta Falcons uniform. Eight hours after that he was back in his baseball uniform. For Sanders, this was just an ordinary workweek.

Deion Sanders was born in Fort Myers, Florida, to Connie and Mims Sanders. His parents divorced when he was two, and he was raised by his mother and stepfather, Willie Knight.

Sanders did not make the varsity football team as a freshman at North Fort Myers High, but joined the varsity unit as a sophomore and made an immediate impact. He played cornerback and returned three interceptions for touchdowns. By his senior year he was also the team's quarterback. In basketball he averaged 24 points per game, and in baseball he was a star pitcher and base stealer.

From the moment Sanders arrived at Florida State University he was a star. As a freshman he returned an interception 100 yards—the longest in Seminoles history. As a senior, he intercepted a pass to preserve victory in the Sugar Bowl. In between he set several school records, including career interception and punt return yards. He starred in other sports as well. One day he played right field in a baseball game, then changed into his track spikes. He ran the third leg of the 4 x 100-meter relay and helped Florida State win the conference title, then hurried back to the diamond to play in the second game of the doubleheader, in which he got the game-winning hit.

Sanders was drafted by the New York Yankees, and he made the big-league club on May 31, 1989. He got his first major-league hit in his first game, and four days later hit his first home run. He called playing in Yankee Stadium "a dream come true."[1] On September 6, 1989, he signed a contract with the Falcons. Sanders was now poised to bring his "Prime Time" act (a nickname given to him by the press) to the national stage. Sanders wore enough gold for a small jewelry shop, and he boasted how he would bring excitement to Atlanta with his flashy play. Some people did not care for such gloating, but it was all an act. "I'm a businessman, and my product is Deion Sanders," he said. "Prime Time is the way I market that product."[2]

In his first pro game, he returned a punt for a touchdown, becoming the first person to hit a major-league home run and score an NFL touchdown in the same week. "In 27 years in this league," said Falcons coach Marion Campbell, "I've never experienced the buzz that goes through a stadium when this guy gets near the football."[3]

Sanders joined the Atlanta Braves in 1991. In the 1992 World Series, he led all players in batting with a .533 average, 2 doubles, 4 runs scored, and 5 stolen bases.

In 1994, Sanders joined the powerhouse San Francisco 49ers in hopes of earning a Super Bowl ring. He got his wish as the 49ers beat the San Diego Chargers, 49–26, in the title game. He joined the Dallas Cowboys the following year and won another ring. He caught the longest pass in that game (a 47-yard reception) as a wide receiver. "The crazy thing about Deion," said high school coach Wade Hummel, "is he could have played in the NBA or won a gold medal in track at the Olympics. He's that great of an athlete."[4]

DEION SANDERS

BORN: August 9, 1967, Fort Myers, Florida.

HIGH SCHOOL: North Fort Myers High School, Fort Myers, Florida.

COLLEGE: Florida State University.

PRO: Baseball: New York Yankees, 1989–1990, Atlanta Braves, 1991–1994, Cincinnati Reds, 1994–1995, 1997, 2001, San Francisco Giants, 1995; Football: Atlanta Falcons, 1989–1993, San Francisco 49ers, 1994–1995, Dallas Cowboys, 1995–1999, Washington Redskins, 2000.

RECORDS: Only athlete to compete in both a Super Bowl and World Series; only NFL player who has recorded both an interception (1994) and a pass reception (1995) in Super Bowl action.

HONORS: High school All-State in football, basketball, and baseball, 1985; two-time college All-American in football, 1987–1988; NFL Defensive Player of the Year, 1994; twice a member of Super Bowl championship teams, 1994–1995.

After college, Sanders played both professional football and baseball. He was given the nickname "Prime Time" by reporters because he entertained fans almost every night of the week.

Internet Address

http://sports.nfl.com/2000/playerhighlights?id=2032

TIGER WOODS

In 2000, Tiger Woods became the youngest golfer ever to win the U.S. Open, British Open, and Canadian Open all in a single year.

TIGER WOODS

TIGER WOODS WAS ON THE FINAL HOLE of the 2000 Canadian Open at the famed Glen Abbey Golf Club. He knew he needed a birdie to win. It usually takes golfers three shots to reach the green on a par-5 hole. Woods can drive the ball so far that he can reach most par-5s in two. But from a fairway bunker, 213 yards from the pin? In the rain?

Woods swung through the sand with a 6-iron and sent the ball screaming toward the green. It sailed over the lake, hit the green on the fly, and stopped just behind it. From there he chipped his third shot to within a foot of the hole. He tapped it in for a birdie to win the tournament. Woods had just become the only player besides Lee Trevino in 1971 to win the U.S. Open, British Open, and Canadian Open in the same year. His 22-under-par total was the lowest in history at Glen Abbey.

Eldrick Woods was born the only child of Earl and Kultida Woods. His father, nicknamed him Tiger after a South Vietnamese soldier who had saved his life during the Vietnam War.

Tiger Woods's golf life began in the family garage. At eleven months old, Tiger stood with his sawed-off putter for the first time, addressed the ball, then wiggled his club twice like his father, and hit the ball.

At age two he played his first hole, taking eight shots to reach the green and three putts to put the ball in the hole. A month later he appeared on TV's *Mike Douglas Show* and putted against famous comedian Bob Hope. At age eight he won his first junior world championship in San Diego, in the ten-and-under division, with a final round of 5-under-par. Woods put a list of golfing great Jack Nicklaus's accomplishments on his bedroom wall. "I want to be the best golfer ever," said Tiger.[1]

As a high school freshman, Woods was featured in *Sports Illustrated* magazine in which he said, "I don't want to be the best black golfer on the Tour. I want to be the best golfer on the Tour."[2] Tiger is part Thai, Chinese, African American, American Indian, and Caucasian. Singling out any one, "is an injustice to all my heritages," he says. "All I can do is be myself."[3] Woods finished high school with a fine 3.79 grade point average and enrolled at Stanford University on a full scholarship. That year he entered and won the first of three straight U.S. Amateur titles.

Woods turned professional in 1996 and finished tied for sixtieth at the Greater Milwaukee Open in his first pro competition. He won the Las Vegas Invitational for his first pro victory.

In early 1997 a commercial was made showing the faces of children of all colors hitting golf balls and saying into the camera "I am Tiger Woods." Woods's image had become global. At famed Augusta National in April he sounded his arrival as the game's dominant force with a stirring twelve-stroke victory over Tom Kite. He became the youngest winner of The Masters Tournament, and his 18-under-par score broke a record held by golf greats Jack Nicklaus and Ray Floyd. "I think winning here is going to do a lot for the game of golf," said Woods. "A lot of kids will start playing it now."[4] In 1999 he won his second Grand Slam major (the PGA Championship). By the year 2000 he owned the golf world, winning three of the four majors (the U.S. Open, British Open, and PGA Championship). At age twenty-four some were already calling him the greatest golfer ever.

TIGER WOODS

BORN: December 30, 1975, Cypress, California.

HIGH SCHOOL: Western High School, Anaheim, California.

COLLEGE: Stanford University.

TURNED PRO: 1996.

RECORDS: First golfer to win three straight U.S. Amateur titles, 1994–1996; won The Masters by largest margin ever (12 strokes), 1997; tour-record earnings of $6,616,585 (nearly twice his nearest competitor), 1999; largest margin of victory in a major (15 shots), U.S. Open, 2000; lowest score in a major (19-under-par), British Open, 2000; won PGA Championship, 2000; won The Masters, 2001.

HONORS: Three-time U.S. Amateur champion, 1994–1996; PGA Tour Rookie of the Year, 1996; *Sports Illustrated's* Sportsman of the Year (youngest to receive honor since gymnast Mary Lou Retton in 1984), 1996; three-time PGA Tour Golfer of the Year, 1997, 1999, 2000.

As a young, accomplished athlete, Tiger Woods inspires young people around the world. While he was still just twenty-four, some people were already calling him the greatest golfer ever.

Internet Address

http://www.tigerwoods.com

CHAPTER NOTES

Kareem Abdul-Jabbar

1. Kareem Abdul-Jabbar, *Kareem* (New York: Random House, 1990), p. 16.

2. Elizabeth A. Schick, ed., *Current Biography* (New York: The H. W. Wilson Company, 1997), p. 1.

Muhammad Ali

1. Thomas Hauser, *Muhammad Ali: His Life and Times* (New York: Touchstone, 1991), p. 67.

2. Charles Moritz, ed., *Current Biography* (New York: The H. W. Wilson Company, 1978), p. 10.

Arthur Ashe

1. Arthur Ashe with Arnold Rampersad, *Days of Grace* (New York: Alfred A. Knopf, 1993), p. 4.

2. Ibid., p. 60.

Jim Brown

1. Charles Moritz, ed., *Current Biography* (New York: The H. W. Wilson Company, 1964), p. 56.

2. Peter King, "Jim Brown," *Sports Illustrated*, September 19, 1994, p. 57.

Michael Jordan

1. Editors, "Michael's Moments," *Boys' Life*, June 1999, p. 31.

2. Ibid., p. 30.

Joe Louis

1. Joe Louis with Edna Rust and Art Rust, Jr., *Joe Louis: My Life* (New York: Harcourt Brace Jovanovich, 1978), p. 141.

2. Robert F. Dorr, "Boxer Joe Louis Symbolized Racial, National Unity in WWII," *Army Times*, July 31, 2000, p. 34.

Jesse Owens

1. Phil Taylor, "Flying in the Face of the Fuhrer," *Sports Illustrated*, November 29, 1999, p. 137.

2. Mat Edelson, "Jesse Owens," *Sport*, December 1999, p. 44.

3. William J. Baker, *Jesse Owens: An American Life* (New York: The Free Press, 1986), p. 19.

4. Ibid., p. 22.

Jackie Robinson

1. Gregg Doyel, "Jackie Robinson," *Sport*, December 1999, p. 48.

2. Anna Rothe, ed., *Current Biography* (New York: The H. W. Wilson Company, 1947), p. 545.

Deion Sanders

1. Judith Graham, ed., *Current Biography* (New York: The H. W. Wilson Company, 1995), p. 506.

2. Ibid., p. 505.

3. Ibid., p. 506.

4. Jeff Savage, Telephone interview with Wade Hummel, August 20, 1994.

Tiger Woods

1. Thomas Boswell, "Save the Tiger," *Golf Magazine*, December 1995, p. 16.

2. Tim Crothers, "Golf Club," *Sports Illustrated*, March 25, 1991, p. 58.

3. Boswell, p. 16.

4. Bob Harig, "Tiger Roars," *St. Petersburg Times*, April 14, 1997, p. 1.

INDEX